I'M A BIG SISTER

by Joanna Cole

Illustrated by Rosalinda Kightley

HARPER FESTIVAL

An Imprint of HarperCollins Publishers

HarperFestival is an imprint of HarperCollins Publishers.

I'm a Big Sister
Text copyright © 1997 by Joanna Cole
Illustrations copyright © 2010 by Rosalinda Kightley
Library of Congress catalog card number: 2009927740
ISBN 978-0-06-190062-4

21   PC   30

Revised edition, 2010

Someone new is at our house.
Do you know who it is?

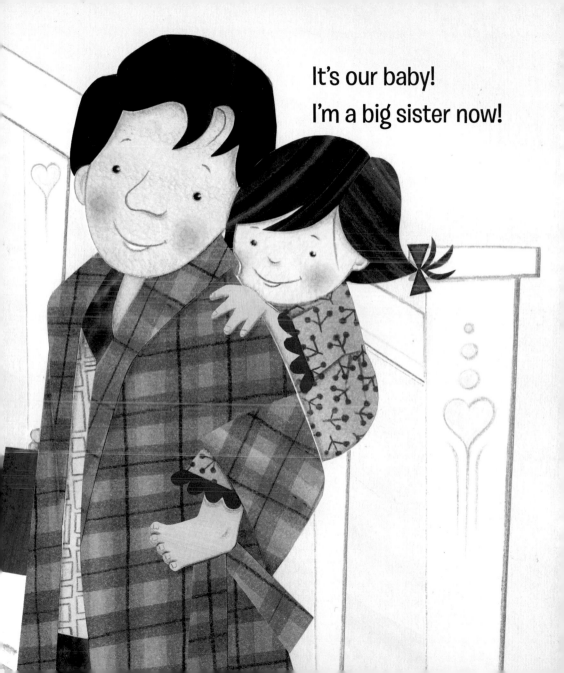

It's our baby!
I'm a big sister now!

The baby is so little. Too little to walk.
Too little to talk. Too little to play with toys.
Too little to eat pizza or apples or ice cream.

Babies like to drink milk.

They like to sleep.

They like to be warm and cozy.

Our baby likes to look at me.

"Look at me, baby.
I'm your big sister."

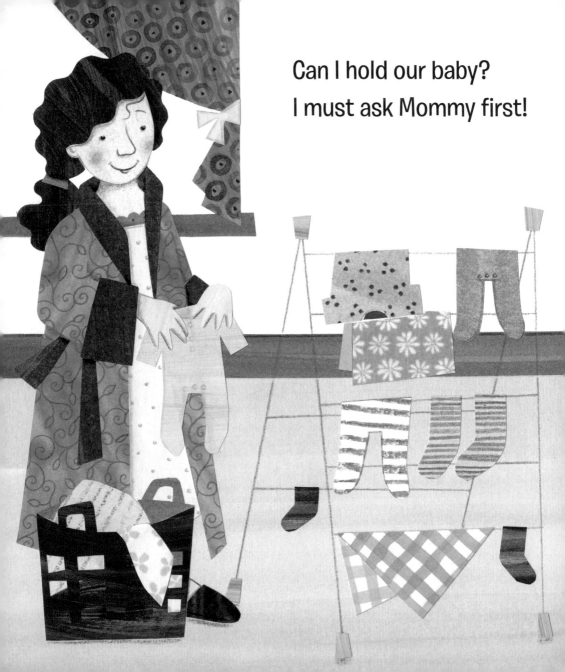

Can I hold our baby?
I must ask Mommy first!

I am gentle with the baby.
I sing a little baby song.
I'm a big sister—I can make
our baby warm and cozy.

Sometimes the baby cries.

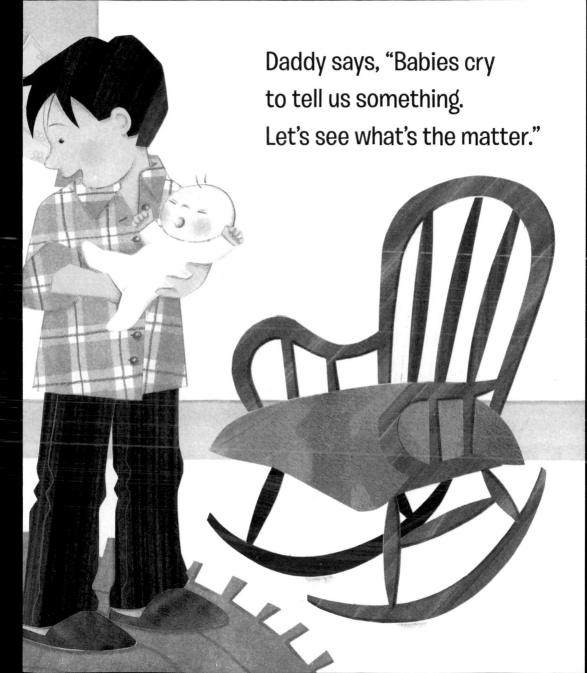

Daddy says, "Babies cry
to tell us something.
Let's see what's the matter."

Oh, it's time to change
the baby's diaper.
It's time for a bottle, too.
I can help—I'm a big sister now.

Mommy and Daddy show me pictures.
Pictures of me when I was a baby.

I was little, too—just like our baby.

Now I am big! It's fun being big.
I can walk. I can talk.

I can play with toys.
I can eat pizza
and apples and ice cream!

Mommy loves me. Daddy loves me.
I am special to them.

I'm the only *me* in the whole world!

I'm special in a new way, too—
I'm a big sister now!

A NOTE TO PARENTS
What a BIG SISTER Needs

When there's a new baby in the house, an older sibling
needs a little extra—a little extra guidance, a little extra
reassurance, and a little extra love. Here are some ways
to help your older child adjust to her new role.

Be sure to set aside time just for your older child. Also, remember to be attentive to her in the presence of the baby, so she feels that she is an important member of the family. Even when you believe you're giving her more than ever, try to understand that it's natural for her to be demanding. Reassure her that your love for her hasn't changed.

Let her know that it's natural for a big sister to feel proud and loving and, at the same time, jealous and angry. Help her express her feelings but communicate clearly that it's not okay to *act* on negative feelings. And don't forget to praise her for good behavior, saying: "It's nice that you are being gentle" and "Thank you for getting the diaper. You're a big help!"

Explain that a newborn has different needs and limitations. That way your older child won't be too disappointed to discover that the baby can't play with her yet. At the same time, show her how the baby can respond to her, so she can begin forming a relationship.

Realize that you can't do everything perfectly all the time. Remember to give yourself a little extra attention, too. Watching the loving bond between your children grow will make up for those frustrating moments.

A caring family has plenty of love to go around!